Scholastic Children's Books,
Euston House,
24 Eversholt Street,
London NW1 1DB, UK

A division of Scholastic Ltd
London ~ New York ~ Toronto ~ Sydney ~ Auckland
Mexico City ~ New Delhi ~ Hong Kong

This book was first published in the US in 2016 by Scholastic Inc.
Published in the UK by Scholastic Ltd, 2016

ISBN 978 1407 17193 7

Cover design by Angela Jun

Printed and bound by CPI Group (UK) Ltd, Croydon, CR0 4YY

2 4 6 8 10 9 7 5 3 1

Papers used by Scholastic Children's Books are made from woods grown in sustainable forests.

www.scholastic.co.uk

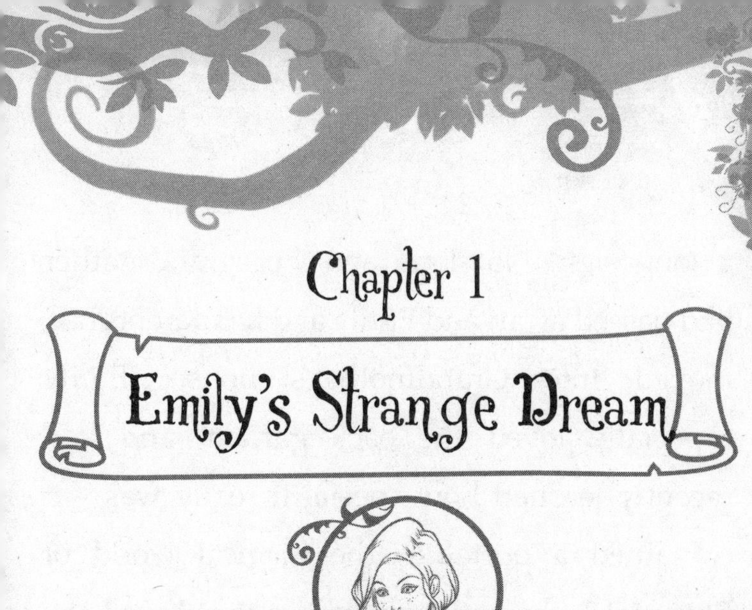

Chapter 1

Emily's Strange Dream

"AUGH!" Emily Jones jolted awake. *Where am I?* she asked herself as she glanced around the dark room, confused and afraid. The last images from her strange dream faded and her heart rate slowly settled. Feeling disoriented, Emily flipped the nearby light switch and was instantly comforted as things became familiar.

She was in her room. In her house.

Emily tugged her duvet up to her chin with

a long sigh. Not long ago, her grandmother had passed away, and Emily and her parents had moved into Grandmother's house. Emily especially loved the back garden, and had recently learned how special it really was – it contained a portal to the magical world of Elvendale! She smiled as she remembered the amazing adventure she'd had there.

And now she was home in her bed. There was no reason for her to be having bad dreams.

Closing her eyes tightly, she tried to recall what it was that had scared her so much.

She could still hear the pained roar. Smell the smoke and see fiery breath. Feel the cold wind created by flapping wings. Sense tremendous loss and sorrow all around her.

Emily's head hurt. The dream felt so real.

Instinctively, Emily reached out and grabbed

hold of the pendant she was wearing. Her grandmother had left her the necklace – it was what had helped her find Elvendale.

She loosened her grip on the blue stone. Suddenly, the medallion began to glow. Emily blinked hard. Was this a sign from Elvendale? On her first trip there, it had glowed just before she found the portal. But it hadn't seemed magical at all since she'd gotten back home.

Emily took another look at the medallion. It wasn't just glowing – the stone's face was a rainbow of swirling colours. She bent even closer, practically pressing her nose against it. There was a faint, fuzzy image within it.

A dragon!

Emily jumped out of bed. She quickly pulled on shorts and a T-shirt. That suffering, howling dragon had been the creature in her dream.

It must live in the land of the elves – and something seemed very wrong. She had to help!

The sky was dark. Emily's parents were asleep. But time passed differently in Elvendale. Last time, she'd been there for days, but when she returned home, only a few minutes had passed.

As she headed to the garden, Emily realized she didn't have any sort of plan, even for opening the portal, but she knew deep in her heart that she needed to go.

The moonlight guided her as she ran down the path, the medallion thumping on her chest with each step.

"I'm coming!" she called out as she reached the old oak tree. The portal was already open – a shimmering, misty blue. Emily didn't think twice. She ran right through, back into the magical land of the elves . . .

Chapter 2

The Adventure Begins

The mountaintop was peaceful and bright as Naida, a water elf, gathered herbs in a basket.

She cut a branch from a yellow bush, and inhaled the scent of its turquoise flowers. They matched her hair. And her dress. And her jewellery. And they smelled amazing. They would be perfect for making lotion for her friends!

Suddenly, a dragon's scream echoed through

the mountains. "What on earth?" she exclaimed. *Where was that coming from?* She paused for a long moment until the cry came again.

Grabbing her basket, Naida hurried towards the sound, climbing over tree trunks and scrambling through bushes. Finally, she reached a small clearing in the woods – which held a dragon queen!

"Ohhh . . ." Naida gasped. The dragon was beautiful – glittering gold with white and blue markings like clouds in a sunny sky.

The dragon screeched again, sounding intensely scared.

It was then that Naida noticed the nest behind the dragon. It held five dragon eggs, each a different colour. One was turquoise with silver glitter, and Naida blinked as the sun glinted off it.

Just as she was about to step out into the clearing, a female figure emerged from the shadow of the tallest tree. This was who the dragon was afraid of.

The figure circled the dragon queen, swinging an enchanted green chain. She whipped it around in the air, and it gave off sparks of magic. Then she lassoed the dragon around the neck.

The dragon shrieked in protest, louder and more fiercely than before, and tossed her head, struggling to escape the chain. The woman only laughed.

Naida had been frozen in horror, but then snapped into action as she felt a wave of sympathy for the dragon and her innocent unhatched babies. She didn't think she could help the dragon, but those eggs were in danger. She had to keep the eggs from being captured!

She tiptoed around the edge of the clearing as quickly as she could, keeping low, as the dragon continued to thrash. She finally reached the nest and carefully set the eggs, one by one, in the bottom of her basket. Just when Naida was about to grab the last egg – the glittering one – the figure saw her.

"Get your hands off those!" she shrieked. Naida could see the figure was an elf, but one who was clearly using her magic for evil: an elf witch. The witch used magic to lift the glittering turquoise egg up out of the nest. Naida jumped for it, but it was too late. The witch plucked it out of the air and screeched, "Now give me the others!"

"No!" Naida yelled back, heart pounding.

She saw the dragon's head was lowered in defeat. "I'll save your babies!" Naida told her. "I promise!" She ran back through the trees as fast as she could.

"I'm telling you, that evil witch almost got me. I barely made it out alive!" Naida was teary and shaking. Her friend Farran, an earth elf, wrapped her in a soft blanket while a fire elf, Azari, stoked the fire to heat a cup of soothing tea. They had been planting seeds in the meadow when Naida arrived in a panic.

"I got your message! I'm here!" Aira, a wind elf, arrived with a gust of wind. She put her hand on Naida's shoulder, and took a peek in her basket. "Wow. Those eggs are amazing! I want to hear the whole story from the beginning."

With a deep breath, Naida repeated what had happened. By the time she finished, she'd stopped shaking, but her grip on the basket was so tight her knuckles ached.

Azari shook her head, tousling her wild red hair. "The witch had the dragon on a chain?"

"Yes! It was like – " Just then, Farran's squirrel friend Miss Spry approached. She circled the elves, sniffing at the basket.

"What's Miss Spry doing here?" Naida asked, pulling the basket away protectively.

Farran listened as Miss Spry huffed and chattered at him – as an earth elf, he could communicate with her. "There was a fire in her forest," he told them. "Her home was destroyed."

"Her home?" Azari exclaimed. "Who would burn down the forest? As a fire elf, I am personally offended. That's not how fire is intended to be used!"

"How awful!" Aira said.

"There's evil in the forest, that's for sure," Naida said.

With a frightened look back at the woods, Miss Spry rushed up into Farran's tree house, chattering away.

"Squirrels . . ." Farran muttered. "How's the saying go? *Can't live with them –* "

"You aren't supposed to live with them," Azari interrupted.

"Well, true," Farran agreed. "But until her home is safe again, she's welcome here."

"What are we going to do?" Naida rubbed her forehead. "The eggs, the dragon queen, the forest fire . . . What is going on?"

"I wish Emily were here." Aira sighed.

"Me, too," Azari said. "I wonder what she would say."

"You don't have to wonder – look!" Farran exclaimed, pointing towards the forest. Emily was running down the path, heading straight for them.

The elves all rushed to her. "We're so happy you're here!" Azari cried, throwing her arms around Emily in a big hug.

Aira and Naida threw themselves into the hug, too. "How'd you get here?" Aira asked at the same time that Naida asked, "Did you know we needed you?"

Farran leapt into the group hug, and everyone toppled over on to the soft, mossy ground.

"Welcome back to Elvendale!" Farran cheered. They all laughed as they untangled themselves, helping one another up. Naida ran to get the basket of eggs.

Emily touched the medallion at her throat. "I had the scariest dream," she said. "It was about Elvendale, and it felt a hundred per cent real."

Naida asked, "Was it about a dragon?"

"Yes!" Emily exclaimed, startled. "How did you know? It was about this poor, trapped dragon that was so beautiful, all white with – "

"Blue and gold markings?" Naida finished.

"Yes!" Emily nodded.

Azari leaned toward Farran and said, "Okay, this is freaky . . ."

"Totally freaky," Emily agreed. She didn't have magical powers like the elves. How had she dreamed about something that was really happening in Elvendale?

She glanced around. It was a warm day, but a chill crept down her spine.

"It wasn't just a dream," Naida said, as if she

y's thoughts. She told Emily
ned in the woods and all about
en. "I saw it."

"The dragon queen is in terrible danger!" Aira added with a shiver.

"Whoa." Farran pointed to Emily's medallion. A shimmering blue glow was coming from the stone.

"Weird, right? This happened at home, too," Emily told them. "I saw an image of the dragon from my dream in it."

"It has more magic in it than just letting you through the portal!" Azari said.

"Maybe it has other secret powers, too," Emily said. She lifted the medallion so they could all look into the stone.

It again showed an image of the dragon queen – an even clearer image than before.

They could see the dragon's pained face in such great detail that Emily nearly dropped the pendant.

"That was awful," Naida said after the image faded.

"Poor dragon," Aira moaned.

Farran ran a hand through his dark hair, and said, "I've heard rumours about an elf witch. She's tall as a mountain and covered in warts."

"Tall? No way, Farran. You have it all wrong," Azari said. "I've heard she's got a humongous head, but the legs of a baby chick."

"Guys, I'm the one who *saw* her!" Naida exclaimed. "She was normal sized . . . just evil." She shook her head. "Wait! I've actually heard and read a lot about this elf witch."

"Well, tell us!" Farran exclaimed.

Naida closed her eyes. "She was an elf who

was born with weak powers. When she was younger, she started comparing herself to other elves – her magic just wasn't very strong, and she became more and more frustrated. But instead of working hard and putting in extra training, she looked for another, easier way to increase her magical powers.

"High in the mountains above the school is the Shadow Fountain. Legend has it that drinking from its waters will bring great magic. So the elf snuck up to it and drank deeply. Power flowed quickly through her veins – she was no longer weak. But the Shadow Fountain's water came with a price. Its power was evil, and the elf did not resist it. She became an elf witch. Since dragons have great power, she became interested in them and used her evil power to turn the dragons against the elves – but it ended up turning the dragons against her as well.

"The witch ran away, and time passed. Everyone thought she was gone for good, but she was really just developing her powers. Recently, she returned and captured the dragons of fire, wind, earth, and water with magical chains – taking them to a hidden castle. If she could harness their power, she could rule all of Elvendale!

"But the wind dragon, earth dragon, and water dragon managed to break free, returning to the Dragon School. The fire dragon still remains the elf witch's prisoner and is under an evil spell. And now she has the even more powerful dragon queen, too – and one of her eggs."

As Naida finished her story, everyone was staring at her in horror.

"How terrible!" Emily cried.

"The poor, poor fire dragon." Azari sniffled. "Wait – what if the fire dragon is being forced to burn the forest?"

"That would be the worst!" Aira said. "Let me call Pluma and ask her if she knows anything about it." She whistled for her bird friend, and had a quick conversation. "Pluma says that Flamy is in the forest." Flamy was a fire fox that they'd met on their last adventure. "He's surveying the damaged part of the woods."

"If anyone can investigate a fire, it's Flamy," Azari said.

"Being fireproof definitely helps with that!" Farran added.

Pluma nestled up close to Aira and chirped in a rapid squawk. Aira turned to Naida. "She says that the animals in Elvendale are afraid."

"We have to find the elf witch and save the dragon queen!" Emily said with a hand on her heart.

Farran was more reluctant. "How about we just return the eggs to their nest? Those other dragons managed to escape the witch. Maybe the dragon queen will escape, too, and come back for them. Besides, do we even know where this elf witch's castle is?" Everyone shook their heads.

Just then, a distant dragon scream echoed through the forest, and Emily's medallion flashed a brilliant blue.

"That doesn't sound promising," Aira said. Glancing at the eggs, she continued. "I don't think the babies will be able to live without their mother when they hatch."

Naida nodded in agreement. "We need to

get the dragon queen's eggs back to her – and free her."

"And help the fire dragon, too!" Azari added.

"It must be the reason I'm here! Let's do it!" Emily cried. Now she knew why she had been called to Elvendale!

Farran started to say, "I – " but at Aira's stern look, muttered, "I'm in."

"All of us are in," Aira said. "But where do we start?"

"The Dragon School!" Naida cried. "We can get some help with these eggs . . ."

Chapter 3

Dragon School

The Dragon School was nestled at the base of a mountain. It had a large field, nice stables for the dragons, and a classroom building that was way bigger than Emily's school back home.

A little dragon soared overhead. Emily shielded her eyes against the sun as she watched it spin in a fast corkscrew dive before straightening out and gently gliding to the ground.

"Hey, look." Naida touched Emily's shoulder. "The little one was tossed into the air by a catapult!"

"That's one way to learn to fly fast!" Emily chuckled. She could see the huge catapult across the field. She wouldn't want to be tossed in the air by that!

Owls circled the elves, escorting them through the school gates and into the training area. There Emily saw an elf watching the little dragon. *He must work at the Dragon School,* she thought. The elf sort of looked like a famous boy-band singer back in her world. The way he tossed his hair made her wonder if he was about to burst into song.

"Miku! Lunch!" he called. As the little dragon flew over, Emily stepped into the trainer's path.

"Hi! I'm Emily Jones," she said to the trainer. "We're hoping you can help us." She saw him do a double take at her ears, but he played it cool and didn't mention them.

The others stepped forward, too, and introduced themselves.

"Nice to meet you all," the trainer said, nodding at them. "I'm the Dragon Trainer. But, unfortunately, I've not had much luck helping anyone lately."

"We heard about the kidnapped dragons," Azari said, giving him a sympathetic look.

"Yeah. Ever since the elf witch captured them, the dragons are all out of sorts. One's still missing, you know," he replied.

"The fire dragon!" Azari told him what they knew already.

While they talked, Emily looked around.

The place felt very desolate. She could see a little pillow bed for Miku in the corner, and four empty dragon beds, which made her sad. Things were not right at the Dragon School.

Naida showed the trainer her basket. "The witch has two dragons now. I saw her capture the dragon queen, and I was able to save almost all her eggs. We want to try to rescue her from the witch."

Naida passed him the basket, and he examined each egg with an expert eye.

As patiently as she could, Emily waited for him to say something. She could tell he was frustrated and sad. She knew how that felt – when her grandmother had passed away, she'd felt like there was a huge hole in her heart. Coming to Elvendale and going on an adventure with her new elf friends had ended up being very healing. She wondered what it would take to heal the hole in the Dragon Trainer's heart.

At last, he spoke. "Follow me," he said, leading them into the school.

They walked down a long hallway, and Emily tried to imagine the school in all its glory. The classrooms must have been filled with dragons of all sizes, colours, and elements, working together . . .

They entered a classroom. "School's in session, but do you see any students?" the trainer asked them, shaking his head. "Trust between dragons and elves is truly broken. It was a delicate balance to begin with – dragons can be trained, but not tamed. They are wild, powerful and independent. And now the elf witch keeps coming back here, trying to steal the other dragons, making it even harder to begin healing the wounds she caused."

"If you keep the eggs," Farran suggested, "once they hatch, you can train the babies while we rescue the queen."

The trainer shook his head. "The school isn't safe for those eggs. The witch is going to be looking for them." He touched each egg gently. "These contain baby dragons of each element: fire, wind, water and earth."

"Oh." Emily nodded. "If the witch has the eggs, she doesn't need to come back here for the dragons. She'll just use the babies for power instead. I get it."

Naida pulled the basket closer, as if to protect it, while Farran took a quick look out of the window.

"Pass me that hourglass, would you?" the

trainer said.

The dusty, sand-filled hourglass was on a shelf next to empty bottles and unused textbooks. Farran handed it to the trainer.

"The eggs look almost ready to hatch, and once the babies are out, they can't survive long without their mother," he said. Holding up the hourglass, he continued. "When the first one hatches, you must turn this over. When each additional egg hatches, flip the hourglass again, and it will magically keep track of time for all of them. The babies must get to their mother before the sand runs out."

Emily's pulse quickened. So much depended on her and her friends!

The trainer seemed to sense her thoughts, and looked right at her. "I have faith in you."

Emily took a deep breath. "We can do this,"

she said. "I know we'll do our best to care for these babies, no matter how hard that might be!"

Farran still looked uneasy. "We're going up against the evil elf witch," he said. "We might not be able to do this on our own."

"I can provide a little help," the trainer said. "I have to stay here right now, but I'll send a message to my friend, the Sky Captain. Go to her inn, and she can take you to a rare book about black magic and dragons that will help guide you to the witch's castle."

"We don't need a book!" Azari proclaimed. "If you know where the elf witch is, just point us in that direction. We're going to set those dragons free!" She grabbed the hourglass and headed for the door. "We've got this, right, Em?"

"Wait, Azari," the trainer called. "You aren't

the first one to try to rescue the fire dragon. I tried – and failed." He rolled up his sleeve so she could see the scars on his arm. "I never even made it to the castle before I had to turn back."

"Oh, fine," Azari huffed. "We can do it your way."

While the trainer explained the route to the Sky Captain's inn, Farran daydreamed, staring out of the window. Suddenly, he spotted a dragon peering around the stables!

Glancing at his friends, he quietly slipped out of the classroom and across the field. It was an earth dragon! Not wanting to show the dragon that he was nervous, Farran approached with his hand outstretched, glowing green with earth magic. Up close, he could see that the dragon had a thorn in his paw.

"Here we go, that's a good boy," Farran

said quietly. He and the dragon were the same element – could they connect magically in a mind-link?

But the dragon refused to bond. He roared and reared up before taking off into the sky.

Frustrated, Farran jogged back to the classroom.

"Hey, where were you?" Aira asked as he came in.

"I just saw an earth dragon out there!" Farran said.

"Are you sure?" the trainer asked. "There haven't been any dragons besides Miku around for a while."

"Of course I'm sure!" Farran retorted. But he could tell the trainer didn't totally believe him.

The trainer shrugged. "Well, I hope you

can do this! If you can defeat the elf witch, we'll have harmony once again." He sounded more optimistic than he had all afternoon. And when he noticed Emily's medallion, he even smiled.

"Emily, your amulet!" It was glowing, and she held it up. The trainer looked deep into her eyes, and said, "You have a very important role in reuniting elves and dragons. I'm certain of it." She nodded, feeling the warmth of the medallion in her hand.

"Now, good luck, friends!" the trainer cried.

They walked away, waving.

"We *can* do this!" Aira announced.

"It's not just about the dragon queen and the fire dragon any more," Azari said.

"Or even just about the eggs," Naida said. "Not entirely."

"We're on a mission to save Elvendale from the elf witch," Farran added.

"Yes . . ." Emily thought about what the trainer had said. "And we'll restore balance between the elves and dragons!"

Their mission was now bigger than any of them had anticipated. They walked on in silence as the weight of their task settled between them.

Chapter 4

The Starlight Inn

High above the school, the path was steep. As they paused to catch their breath, Emily looked down. She could still see the Dragon Trainer in the schoolyard – he was the size of an ant from this distance. A tiny Miku went soaring across the yard, shrieking with joy.

Farran told his friends about the thorn in the earth dragon's paw. "I felt so bad that I wasn't able to help him," he said. Emily was sad that the dragons didn't trust elves enough to even get a splinter out. She remembered when a friend at school had told another girl one of Emily's secrets, breaking her trust, and how much that had hurt. But they had made up. She hoped that the elves and dragons could, too.

"Let's keep moving towards the inn!" Azari urged them.

They started walking again. Aira and Azari were in the lead, with Farran and Naida close behind, and Emily in the rear. She was watching her step carefully on the uneven ground. Suddenly, Aira shouted. "Aaaaagh!"

She'd just taken the first step on to a crumbling staircase built into the side of the mountain when chunks of the stairs gave way. Next to the stairs was just a steep, long drop to a canyon below.

Farran grabbed Aira's hand to steady her, then refused to let go even after she'd firmly planted her feet. "It's safer this way," he told her.

Emily thought that was a good idea, and suggested they all hold hands in a chain. Everyone was happy to comply. Aira calmed the wind around them with her magic, and Farran magically called up roots from the mountainside to form a safety net around them as they slowly moved forward.

They'd gone about halfway up the stairs when they encountered a small boulder blocking the path. One by one, they stepped over it, but then Naida tripped.

"Oh no!" Her voice echoed. One of the dragon's eggs flew out of the basket and tumbled through the air towards a cliff edge. "The egg!"

Emily gasped as Farran made an amazing dive for it, the roots magically helping support him. He slid down a few decaying steps, reaching out precariously over the edge of the cliff – and grabbed it.

"No sweat," Farran joked as they tugged him to safety. Everyone caught their breath for a moment.

"Whew!" Emily said, trying not to dwell on what had just happened. "C'mon, it can't be much further . . ." They just had to keep moving, If she thought too much about the danger, she'd probably give up and find a portal home.

One foot in front of the other. Breathe in and out. Don't look at the edge, Emily told herself.

They continued upward.

As the sun went down, Azari pulled out some matches, lit a fire, and manipulated it into a bright orb to lead them.

One foot . . . Breathe . . .

Emily was so caught up in taking each step safely, she didn't notice when they'd finally reached the top.

"Look!" Farran pointed at lights on the crest of the next hill.

"That's it! We're here, guys!" Azari called. Emily laughed at herself for being nervous. Of course they'd made it . . . and except for the parts where Aira nearly fell off a cliff and Naida nearly lost an egg, it had been easy!

Naida held the basket close as they all broke into a run towards the warm lights of the inn.

The sign above the door said, “Starlight Inn.”

“It sure looks starlit to me!” Azari said as they entered the large stone building.

The first thing Emily noticed were the stars twinkling through the windows.

“It’s so cozy in here, just like my cave!” Naida gushed.

Aira took a deep breath and said, “I’m just glad I can’t fall off a cliff in here. There are chairs with cushions!” She plopped down on the couch and propped her feet up on a small table.

Farran was gazing around and let out a yelp as he bumped into something. It was a girl elf. He raised his hands in a defensive stance as he turned to face her. “Friend or foe?” he asked.

“Somebody should really look where he’s going,” she said, hands on hips.

"Oh! Uh, hey. I'm sorry," he said, embarrassed. "I mean, I'm Farran. You're . . . You look nice. Thank you!"

Emily held out her hand towards the elf. "You must be the Sky Captain. Thank you for hosting us here."

The Sky Captain shook Emily's hand, then gave Farran a hearty slap on the back. "Welcome to my home, and the best inn around!" she said. Farran gave a weak chuckle.

"This place is so impressive," Naida said, her voice filled with awe.

Azari stepped forward and gestured towards Naida's basket. "We actually are in a big hurry. Once these eggs hatch, our mission becomes life or death!"

Emily nodded. Azari was right. They didn't have any time to waste.

"The Dragon Trainer told me what was up." The Sky Captain looked out of the window and pointed at twinkling lights in the far distance. "That's your next stop. Too bad you can't fly!"

"I can!" Aira said. "I made these mechanical wings that allow me to—"

The Sky Captain interrupted, continuing her own train of thought. "I mean, wouldn't that be amazing? Who made up the rule that earth elves had to stay on land? Booorriiing! Right, Farran?"

Farran, usually a big talker, didn't have a response. "Uh, well, ha . . . I say that all the time, too!" he said.

"No, you don't!" Azari said, eyebrow raised.

"Well . . . whatever," Farran replied.

The Sky Captain turned to Aira. "Mechanical wings are okay, but they won't get you far. I have an airship."

Naida's eyes grew big. "Wow, an airship *and* your own inn?"

"So what? You have a boat," Aira told Naida. "That's amazing, too. And you live in a cave. And have water powers. We all have things that—"

The Sky Captain continued, "My airship's pretty sweet. It has . . ." She went on and on.

Emily held back a chuckle and looked around as Farran kept trying to interrupt the Sky Captain. On the other side of the inn's reception area, two elves passed through. Emily could hear them talking to each other.

"Yeah," the shorter one was saying. "Two dragons, huge. One was in chains, and the other was in a helmet. Poor things."

The other asked, "And you say a witch had them?"

The first elf straightened his work hat. "Yeah! She was leading them into the Shadow Lands."

That was all Emily caught before they left the room. A knot formed in her stomach. She asked the others, "Did you hear that?"

None of them had. Emily relayed the conversation, and the Sky Captain said, "So . . . the hidden castle must be in the Shadow Lands. Guess we know where we're heading after we get that book, huh?"

"We?" Farran asked.

"Yep! I'm coming along," she said. "I promised the Dragon Trainer I'd help you, and so I will!"

"Yippee!" Farran exclaimed, blushing when Aira rolled her eyes.

"So, where is this book?" Naida asked.

"It's in the ancient library at the Secret

Marketplace, which is beyond the mountains of Diamond Peaks and somewhere near the Forgotten Valley—"

"Whoa, hang on! Look!" Naida exclaimed as one of the eggs in her basket began to wobble. She took out the egg and tenderly set it on the floor. They all gathered around, and for the first time since they'd arrived at the inn, the Sky Captain was speechless.

The egg rolled around to the left, then circled to the right. A crack appeared in the shell. It was small at first, but grew bigger, and a claw popped out. The claw stretched out and chunks of eggshell fell aside until a whole foot emerged. Then another foot. Finally, with a mighty *CRACK*, the egg burst open.

Emily's heart swelled. A dragon egg was hatching right in front of her!

"Awww! She's a baby fire dragon!" Azari exclaimed. She leaned in and tried to mind-link, but it didn't work. Then Azari reached out and stroked the dragon's little back scales, but she began to make sad-sounding squeaks, and wouldn't stop.

Emily watched Azari grow frustrated. She wished she knew how to comfort a baby dragon. Did they make dragon pacifiers?

Azari turned back towards them. "What do I do?"

"I could sing," Aira suggested. She started to hum, and the baby dragon made even louder noises.

"Stop!" everyone said at once. Aira was a terrible singer!

"Let me try," Emily said, tenderly approaching the baby, which shrieked, emitting smoke and little sparks.

"Don't let that thing burn down the inn!" the Sky Captain warned.

"Hey, little girl." Emily leaned over the dragon, smiling. Her medallion swung down in front of the dragon, calming the creature. Moving slowly, Emily was able to pick up the dragon and cradle her in her arms.

"Somebody's got the magic touch," the Sky Captain said.

Farran said, "Thanks!" Then he blushed. "Oh, you mean Emily. Yeah."

"It wasn't me," Emily said. "It's the medallion that calmed her. I think she's able to somehow sense her mother through it."

"We've got to get her to her mother in real life!" Azari handed the hourglass to Naida, who flipped it over. The grains of grey sand began to trickle down to the bottom half.

The countdown had begun.

Chapter 5

The Secret Marketplace

As the sun rose above them, the Sky Captain led Emily and the elves through rugged mountains and valleys. Emily had the baby dragon in her arms. Naida had the basket of eggs, and kept nervously glancing at the hourglass. It was perched in the basket, a constant reminder for them to move quickly. As the path grew steeper, Emily was glad they had a guide who knew the route.

Aira slowed to walk with Emily and Naida.

"Check out Farran, blah-blah-blah-ing away to the Sky Captain," Aira complained. "Will he ever stop talking?"

"It must be an earth elf thing," Emily said, giggling. "It's nice that Farran found someone who—"

"Guys, careful on this next passage!" the Sky Captain called back at them.

"Okay," Azari said. "You don't have to warn us. We're always caref—" She swallowed her words when they turned a sharp corner. "Whoa." The only way to continue was to climb tall ladders extending up the steep mountain face.

The Sky Captain easily scrambled up one ladder, then jumped and grabbed the rock face with her bare hands. "See, no trouble at all!"

she called as she pulled herself from rock to rock, using earth magic to help her on particularly tricky spots. Emily's heart was in her throat as she watched, knowing that a single misstep would be terrible. But soon the Sky Captain was up on a flat area above them all. "Come on up!" she said. "It's awesome – feels like I'm flying!"

Farran was frozen at the base of the ladders.

"Are you going first?" Aira asked.

"Nope," he said, edging backward. "I'm going back to the inn."

"Come on, Farran," the Sky Captain called from the top. "Show them all what an earth elf can do!"

"Bah . . ." Farran groaned as placed his foot on to the first ladder rung.

"Nothing more to say, Farran?" Aira teased.

Lips pressed tightly together, he silently worked his way up the sheer rock face. Aira followed close behind.

Emily gulped as she looked up. She was still holding the baby fire dragon, and she was nervous about climbing the ladder with her. But she knew she had to do it. Rung by rung, she climbed. Her arms tired quickly as she held on to both the rungs and the baby. Her legs felt rubbery. It was much more difficult than any of the gymnastics she'd done in her school PE class back at home!

Home. It seemed so far from where she was right now. She missed her mum and dad, but was glad to be with her friends in Elvendale. Even though she was struggling right now, she knew what they were doing was important.

The dragon baby in her arms gave a little

squawk as Emily finally reached the top. "We'll get you to your mum," she promised.

Azari was the last one up, and they all cheered as she came over the ledge.

But soon they reached a rickety bridge across a deep ravine.

"No way!" Farran shook his head. "This is my limit. I climbed the ladder, but I cannot cross that bridge. I can't even see the bottom down there!" The rotten planks swayed when the wind blew, and Emily felt uneasy, too.

"Is this how an earth elf behaves?" Aira mocked him.

"Yes," he said. "I want my feet on the ground – flat, solid ground."

"You can't back out now!" the Sky Captain said. "We're almost there." She skittered across the bridge without glancing back. "Hold steady, guys. Don't step on any loose planks, and whatever you do, don't look down. Come on, Farran."

"After you," Aira said, stepping out of his way.

With a frown, he started out after the Sky Captain.

Inch by inch, the whole group tensely made their way across. When a quick breeze rattled the bridge, Emily looked down at the baby dragon. "You okay, little one?" The dragon grunted back at her.

Soon they'd all reached the other side.

"That wasn't so bad," Farran said. He was about to sit down to rest when Azari called, "Look!" Not so far in the distance were brightly coloured tents and flags that billowed in the breeze. "The Secret Marketplace!"

Emily couldn't stop turning her head as they walked into the Secret Marketplace. There were so many sights and sounds – and the entire market was run by animals! She jumped aside as a deer wheeled a cart of pumpkins past her.

"As far as secrets go, this is a pretty cool one!" Farran admitted, craning his neck to try to see everything.

They were moving through a crowded alley when Flamy rushed by, sweeping his long tail against Azari's feet.

Azari was surprised to see him. "Flamy! Hey, little dude! Wait!"

Emily strained to listen as the fire fox growled at Azari repeatedly while she nodded, frowning. Finally, she waved goodbye, and Flamy took off, running under a cart filled with fabulously coloured fabric, buttons and beads.

"What did he say?" Emily asked as they followed the Sky Captain.

"He's on a mission to warn Elvendale's animals," Azari said with a long sigh. "We were right! The elf witch is using the fire dragon to burn the trees and force animals to leave the forest. She's taking over everything!"

"What if she goes after the water next?" Naida gasped. "She could force the dragon to pollute the rivers, make tsunamis or destroy the sea life!"

"Or what about the wind?" Aira said. "She'd have control of the weather!"

"Oh no!" Farran said. "If she had an earth dragon . . ." He shook his head in a panic. "I can't even think about it! That evil witch is going to destroy Elvendale."

"Not if we stop her first," Emily said.

Azari looked at the baby fire dragon and then raised her hands above her head and declared, "All right! Let's get that book!"

The Sky Captain took them into a building, through a maze of hallways, through several doors, and even through some sort of window. Finally, they found themselves in a library. The Sky Captain pushed aside some old books on an ordinary-looking shelf, revealing a tiny hidden tree behind it. She motioned for Farran to join her, and together they used their earth powers to open the tree . . . revealing the book they'd come for.

Emily was certain they never would have found it without the Sky Captain.

"I used to come here as a kid," the Sky

Captain explained. "I know every book in the library!"

"This place is amazing," Naida told her. "I love stories. Are there any books here about mermaids, or tidal patterns, or dolphins?"

"Yes to all," the Sky Captain said.

"Wow. I wish we had more time," Naida said. She glanced at the hourglass, still trickling away, and sighed. "But we don't."

The Sky Captain held the book gently. It looked old and fragile, and its cover was so grey and faded the text was illegible.

"That's it?" Azari asked. She flashed a glance at Emily. "Seriously? That tattered paperweight is going to help us? It just looks like one more thing we have to carry . . ."

The Sky Captain blew off the dust. "This is the book the Dragon Trainer told you about. It's loaded with info about dragons and black magic, and it will guide us through the Shadow Lands. So, I'd say it's pretty valuable!" She handed the book to Emily.

Whoosh! An owl swept through the library window and dropped a letter into the Sky Captain's hands.

"This is from the Dragon Trainer." She read it quickly. "He needs me to meet him at the Dragon Sanctuary right now."

"What's up?" Farran asked. "Can we help?"

"You already have something important to do," the Sky Captain said, hurrying to the door. "I've got to go. You'll have to head to the Shadow Lands without me."

"No problemo!" Azari said. "We've got this."

"I'm sure you have!" the Sky Captain said. "But you're about to face even higher mountains and narrower bridges than we've already encountered, and more of those eggs are going to hatch. Stay safe, you guys."

Emily shouted, "Thanks!" as the Sky Captain disappeared from sight.

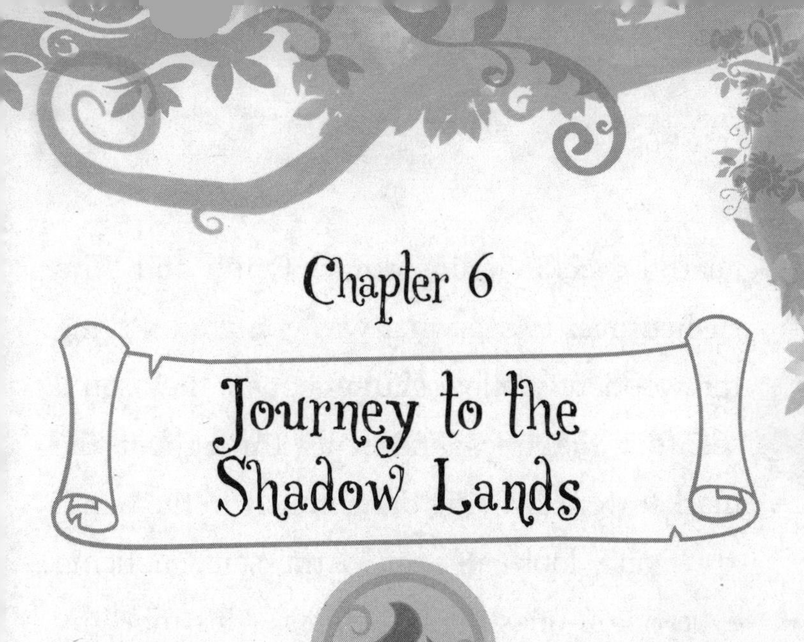

Chapter 6

Journey to the Shadow Lands

"Anyone remember how we got in here?" Farran asked, clicking his tongue. "I don't even know if I could make it out of the library, let alone out of the Secret Marketplace!"

Emily didn't have a clue. Had any of the other elves been paying better attention?

"OOF!" Farran jumped back when a great gust of wind smashed the library window shut, nearly knocking him down. Emily and Aira rushed over to see what was going on. Prying the wooden window shutters open, they could see that the trees and tents throughout the market were swaying dangerously in the wind.

"Don't look at me," Aira said, noticing everyone's questioning stares. "It's not my wind."

"Who's is it, then?" Naida asked, squeezing next to Emily to peer outside. A green blur swept by the window. "Ohhh."

The earth dragon swooped down on the Secret Marketplace, overturning the cart of pumpkins they'd seen earlier. With a mighty roar, he ate them all in one bite.

"Whoa!" Azari said. "I knew he was hungry!"

Then the dragon sat down, smashing a vegetable cart. Onions and carrots rolled out into the street. He licked at his paw with a long, flickering tongue.

"You guys! This is the dragon I tried to help earlier!" said Farran.

"Can you try to help him again?" Emily asked. "I think he's still got the splinter."

"It's no use – I'm sure he won't let me," Farran replied.

"But he just ate," Azari said, giving Farran a little shove toward the door. "Maybe he'll be more receptive with a full tummy."

Straightening his shoulders and standing tall, Farran strode confidently to the door (though Emily could have sworn she could hear him muttering about this being the last time he ever left the meadow).

It wasn't hard to find the dragon – they just followed the sound of his roars.

The deer that owned the vegetable cart was hiding behind a fruit stand.

"Farran will help the dragon," Emily told her.

Farran took a breath and moved forward. The dragon raised his head and snorted. Farran stopped.

"He's probably just nervous, too!" Azari assured him.

"Maybe . . ." he said, sounding uncertain. But he raised his arms and let earth energy flow through him, concentrating on making everything calm.

Farran touched the dragon's paw, but jumped away as the dragon let out a mighty roar.

"Forget it!" Farran shook his head. "I can't do this."

Emily touched her Grandmother's medallion, and said, "Imagine how terrible his foot feels. You're the only one who can end his pain."

"You're right," Farran said with a sigh. He turned back to the dragon and tried again. This time, though, he used his earth magic to grow some gigantic flowers around the dragon's head, distracting him. Then he managed to grab the splinter and very gently pull it out.

The dragon exhaled a long, warm puff of steam over Farran. With a much less ferocious roar, he stretched his wings and took off into the air. The sound of a horn blasted in the distance.

The girls rushed towards Farran, cheering and high-fiving.

"You did it!" Aira gave Farran a big hug.

"I was able to bond with him!" Farran cried, awed. "His name is Thorne."

Just then, an engine whirred above them. It was the Sky Captain soaring past in her airship!

"The Shadow Lands are that-a-way! Get that witch!" she called, then flew off in the same direction as the earth dragon.

The animals of the Secret Marketplace were grateful that the dragon was gone. Before Emily and the elves left, they were given fresh fruit, vegetables and bread for the journey as a thank-you.

Aira started reading the special book as they walked.

Naida held up the hourglass. Half the sand was already gone. "I hope we can make it!"

"Anything helpful in the book?" Emily asked Aira.

"A few things . . . It says there'll be a special visitor to help restore balance between dragons and elves. That must mean Emily," she said, smiling at Emily. "There's also a great map to the Shadow Lands." Then she stopped and pointed towards a glowing volcano in the distance, capped with white clouds.

Aira flipped a page in the book, then studied the volcano more intently. "Very interesting."

Naida said, "I've seen pictures of that mountain before. What is it?"

"It's the Dragon Sanctuary," Aira answered. "It's a very special meeting place for the dragons – they gather there for important events and discussions. That's where the Sky Captain was heading."

"Like a dragon holiday spot?" Azari asked.

"It looks like there are lots of plants and waterfalls on it."

"A holiday sounds great," Farran said, sighing wistfully.

Azari smirked. "First, we need to see an evil witch about some dragons . . ."

"Darn," Farran said. "It was worth a try!"

Aira closed the book with a snap. "C'mon, let's get these babies to their mum!"

The bridge to the Shadow Lands was in worse shape than the bridge they'd crossed on the way to the Secret Marketplace, and it was even higher up. And yet, Emily was feeling brave. They'd come this far already. She *would* cross this bridge. As long as she didn't look down, it was going to be fine. "You guys ready?"

Naida peeked down. "I'll be really happy

once we don't have to cross any more bridges!"

They lined up in single file to cross.

The baby dragon choked and coughed, spewing a few weak sparks and some smoke.

"We have to hurry!" Azari said anxiously.

A gust of wind rattled the bridge. Aira said, "I wish I could make the breeze stop – it would make this much easier!"

"Uh, guys," Emily said, pointing in the direction they were going. Two huge dragons were heading right towards them! It was the wind dragon and the fire dragon – and they seemed to be fighting. The fire dragon had a helmet on her head.

The two dragons shrieked, clawing at the air as they circled each other, blowing gusts of wind and fire.

They separated, and the fire dragon flew

upward, green eyes flashing anger. Then she turned suddenly, diving straight towards the bridge!

"Where'd the wind dragon go?" Aira shouted, looking around frantically. Before they could locate her, the fire dragon slammed hard into the bridge.

"Aaaaaaaaaaahhhh!" they all screamed. The bridge shook violently . . . but didn't break.

Emily and the elves clung to one another, terrified and frozen in place.

"Stay together, and don't look down," Emily said. "We have to get to the other side! Just one step at a time . . ."

Naida was having trouble with the basket of eggs, which swung wildly in the breeze.

"I'll take an egg," Aira told her.

"Give me one, too," Farran said.

Azari took the hourglass and the book and put them in her pack. Emily had the baby fire dragon.

They inched forward. The other side seemed impossibly far away.

The fire dragon looked dazed from her fall and was holding her wing. She settled behind them on the bridge.

"I'm going to try to mind-link with her," Azari said.

Naida argued, "Azari, no! She's evil."

"I'm a fire elf, and she's a fire dragon – and she's not evil, she's under an evil spell," Azari insisted. "You guys can go on ahead if you want." They all refused.

"Please be careful, Azari!" Farran said.

The huge dragon blew angry fire at Azari, but Azari used her magic, raising her hands and deflecting the flames.

After another minute she turned back towards them. "It's not working. I think that helmet is blocking my mind-link – it's controlling the dragon somehow!"

"Then let's get out of here!" Farran cried. They all started moving as fast as they could towards the other side.

The bridge was swinging violently. Aira lost her balance . . . and dropped the egg she was holding. It landed on a wooden slat, bounced, then went over the side, falling into the abyss below.

Without hesitating, Aira leapt after the egg, soaring down into the clouds.

"Aira, no!" Naida screamed. Her cry echoed through the valley.

Emily leaned over, panicked. What had just happened? Could Aira survive that leap? The baby fire dragon could tell something was wrong, and flailed in Emily's arms, almost slipping out.

"Aira! AIRAAAA!" Azari called out into the wind. There was no sound from below. "We have to go after her. We have to save her!"

Everyone was in shock.

But suddenly the fire dragon reared up and moved towards them, shooting flames.

"She's going to hurt us!" Naida screamed, hysterical.

"We've got to move, or we'll be toast!" Emily yelled. She leapt into action, barely thinking of the danger they were in before focusing on what she needed to do. She passed the baby dragon to Farran. "I have to get on the fire dragon!" she yelled. Her friends turned their full attention towards her.

As the fire dragon came close, Farran used his magic to bind the dragon's legs with roots, Azari used her magic to block the dragon's flames, and Naida used her magic to create a protective water bubble around Emily. With all of that help, Emily had time to make a running leap – right on to the dragon's back!

"Aaaaaaahhh!" Emily struggled to pull herself up the dragon's neck, adrenaline rushing through her veins. She grabbed the fire dragon's evil helmet, tearing it off her head. The fire dragon slowed her movements, confused, and Emily jumped back on to the bridge.

The dragon shook her head, realizing the helmet was gone. She blinked slowly and curled her lips.

"Either she's going to eat us or she's smiling," Farran said.

"Smiling!" Azari was certain. "Emily! You freed her!"

They were all rejoicing when a sudden *crack* ended the excitement.

"The bridge!" Naida grabbed her basket and hurried towards the other side of the ravine. Farran and Azari were right behind her – but Emily's foot got caught in a loose plank.

"Emily!" Azari cried, turning back towards her. But before she could take a step, the fire dragon scooped Emily up in her paw, then pushed the elves to safety with her tail just as the bridge collapsed.

"That was way too close," Naida said, taking big gulping breaths. Farran set his egg back in her basket with the other remaining egg.

"We couldn't have made it without the fire dragon," Emily said, smiling up at her.

"Look, look!" Azari cried, pointing at the eggs. One of them wiggled and cracked. A moment later, out popped a baby wind dragon.

"Oh, my!" Naida exclaimed. "A wind dragon! She's adorable!"

The baby immediately started to howl. Naida tried to use some water magic to soothe it, by creating a little rain shower from a nearby puddle. But the baby dragon continued to whine.

Farran brought over the baby fire dragon. "Look. Here's your sister!"

The wind dragon was still upset.

"Let me try with my medallion," Emily said. Thinking of her grandmother, Emily held the medallion over the baby dragon. It began to glow, and the baby reached towards it with a tiny claw. Emily was able to cuddle her close.

Naida glanced at the hourglass. "That's another one on the clock."

Azari held the baby fire dragon, who was weakening. She could barely raise her head. "We have to get to that castle soon!"

"But what about Aira?" Farran asked, glancing down into the deep ravine. "Are we terrible friends for not jumping after her?"

Emily felt sick to her stomach. How could they leave Aira behind? Was Aira okay? She hoped with all her might that she was. And they had to keep moving forward.

Emily touched Farran's hand. Putting on a brave face, she said, "We have to hope for the best. Aira is strong, she's smart, and the clouds and wind are her allies. We wouldn't have survived if we'd gone after her." She thought about her parents back home, and how they would feel if she never returned. It was just one more reason they had to succeed.

With no time to rest, the group pressed on. But now, the great fire dragon led the way, though her wing was badly injured.

They could finally see the silhouette of a castle looming in the distance.

"That's where we need to be," Emily said. "We'll stop the witch so she can no longer spread her evil through Elvendale!"

Chapter 7
The Shadow Fountain

Aira was lying on a ledge far below the bridge. When she'd leapt, she'd called up a soft wind to carry her down gently and give her a smooth landing in a soft, mossy patch. She sat up, checking herself and the egg for anything broken. They were both fine. The moss had made a nice cushion.

But she was rattled and worried. There was no way to tell the others she was fine, and no easy way to get back up to them. She was going to have to go on alone. Aira didn't mind being alone in her own workshop, but being alone here, wherever she was – with a dragon egg – was another story.

A shadow appeared overhead. Aira slowly looked up . . . right into the wind dragon's eyes.

She gasped. She'd never be able to outrun a dragon – so she decided to try to mind-link with her. It was worth a try . . .

"Hi there, beauty! I'm Aira, a wind elf, just like you're a wind dragon! Together we can – "

The dragon roared at Aira and swished her heavy tail around. Aira ducked her head just in time.

"Whoa, hey, it's okay – we can bond later. Take all the time you need." Aira backed away slowly, taking deep breaths to calm her pounding heart.

The dragon blew a light gust of wind at her, then moved closer.

She didn't seem dangerous. Aira took a few tiny steps forward. The dragon bent low, and – *WHUMP* – scooped Aira up with her tail, plopping her down on her back!

"Whoa!" Aira tried to control her shock. "What is . . . Okay. This will be okay." She settled on to the dragon's back and held on tight to her scales. "Let's go find my friends," she said.

In the distance, a horn blared. The sound echoed through the canyon.

The wind dragon flapped her huge wings and lifted into the air. But they weren't flying back towards the bridge. The dragon was taking them in the direction of the horn blast.

"Aaah! Aaah! Aaaaaahhh!" Aira screamed as they got higher and higher. "Where are we gooooooing?!"

"We have to stop for the night," Emily told the others. It was dark on the mountain and they were moving slowly.

The fire dragon's injury seemed to be getting worse. "I think her wing is broken," Azari said. "She's not complaining, but I think she's in a lot of pain."

"And the fire baby is taking shallow breaths," Emily added.

Naida took the book and skimmed through its pages. "We're going in the right direction. But it looks like we're still a bit of a distance away."

"Okay, then. Let's camp for the night," Farran said. "I promise I won't snore!"

"Oh, don't promise," Azari said. "We've all camped near you before!"

He laughed. "You'll be happy when I scare the mountain monsters away!"

"There are no mountain monsters," Azari said, shivering. "We're too high up, and it's too cold. Who would want to live here?"

"Exactly." Farran smiled. "You can thank me later." He pointed out a nearby cave. "That looks comfy!"

They set up camp. Emily cooed quietly over the baby dragons, swinging her medallion. Naida sat with the book, scanning the pages, searching for any information they might need. After a while, she shut the cover. "If Aira was here, I'm sure she'd be reading this instead of me." She sighed. "Where, um . . . where do you think she is right now?"

Azari's eyes flashed. She stood up and paced the cave. "She's GONE! That's where she is." She stared hard at the large fire dragon. "It's your fault!"

The fire dragon wiggled back into the shadows and melted into the darkness.

Emily got up and went to Azari. "Hey!" she said. "The dragon was under a spell and didn't know what she was doing!"

Azari countered, "Spell, shmell! She's as evil as the witch."

"Whoa." Naida jumped between Emily and Azari. "Have you both lost your minds? How can you fight when . . ." Naida stomped her foot. "Actually, go ahead and fight. At least you don't keep wanting to turn back, like Farran."

Farran leapt up. "So what if I like my home?

What's wrong with that?" He gave them each a hard look. "What is even going on right now?"

Naida rolled her eyes and spun around on her heel, then stopped. "Do you guys hear that?" She tipped her head. "It's water."

"Water? I don't hear any—" Emily started.

Azari interrupted. "Of course you don't! You have such little ears!"

"My ears are—" Emily started shouting back when Farran pushed past them, knocking into Naida. He walked out of the cave and down a rough, overgrown path.

"Let's follow him," Emily said to the others.

"Why?" Azari asked, hands on hips. "If he wants to get lost in the dark, let him."

A nagging feeling in Emily told her this was all wrong. These were her friends, and they were in the middle of an important mission.

Why were they fighting? Her chest felt tight with anger and confusion.

"Stay here if you want," she told Azari. "I'm going after him."

They all ended up following him, except for the fire dragon, who was still sulking in the corner. They walked in a prickly silence.

They found Farran at the end of a short path, standing near a small fountain. The water trickled over smooth rocks into a natural pond.

"Told you there was water," Naida muttered.

Azari let out a big sigh.

Emily had a bad feeling about the fountain. She tried to figure out why as Naida and Azari started arguing again.

But Farran wasn't just looking at the fountain any more. He was moving towards it with glassy eyes, as if it was controlling him. He scooped up some water in his hands and raised it to his mouth . . .

"No!" Emily dove between Azari and Naida, tackling Farran to the ground and knocking his hands away. "Farran, no!"

"You can't stop me . . ." he said, reaching for the water again. The fountain sprayed a gush of dark, murky water at Emily, pushing her back.

"Whoa! It's alive!" Emily cried.

Naida's eyes flickered, then cleared. "That is not natural! And I can't stop it with my water magic!" She got the book out, and flipped through. "Look!" She handed the book to Emily.

Emily read, "*Water can be beautiful, but sometimes it's for show. Remember your surroundings and the presence of your foe.*" It was a warning. Emily felt her alarm grow as she realized how much evil magic they were near.

"We have to get away from here!" Emily grabbed Farran around the waist and pulled him backward, and Naida tugged on Azari's arm. But Azari and Farran had started bickering again, and were each trying to get to the enchanted fountain.

Emily and Naida also felt the pull – the fountain's water looked clear and enticing. "The fountain might be too strong for us!" Naida said.

Just then, the fire dragon appeared. She wrapped her tail around Emily and the elves, gently pulling them away from the fountain. It sprayed green water after them.

As soon as they were a good distance away, their minds all felt clearer.

"That has to be the Shadow Fountain that turned the elf witch evil!" Naida said.

"It sure has some strong magic," Azari said.

"I'm sorry I was so angry before – though I think the fountain had something to do with it." She stroked the fire dragon's leg in apology.

"I'm sorry, too," Farran told them. "No wonder the elf witch is so evil! Can you imagine what would have happened if Azari had drunk the water?" He smiled. "Good thing I was there to stop her!"

Emily and Naida looked at each other and laughed.

"Yeah," Emily said, rolling her eyes. "Good thing."

It was still dark, but they all agreed they needed to get far away from the fountain as soon as possible. So they kept moving until they found a clearing to camp in. Azari built a new fire and they all gathered around.

"Come here." Azari beckoned to the fire

dragon, trying to mind-link. "I know what happened at the bridge wasn't your fault. And you saved us all at the fountain." She leaned against the dragon's tail and said softly, "Thank you." A moment later, Azari had fully mind-linked with the fire dragon. "Her name is Zonya!" she called happily.

Emily smiled, then sighed. It had been a hard, long day – one of the most difficult she had ever faced. She thought back to the Secret Marketplace . . . So much had happened since then. Emily yawned. They had to take a break or they'd start bickering again, even without the fountain's evil magic.

With another yawn, Emily snuggled between the two baby dragons. "I'm sure we'll make better time in the morning. Let's get some sleep."

Chapter 8

The Witch's Castle

Emily and the elves were standing outside the castle. They'd made it. Now, only a narrow bridge over a wide moat stood in the way of the imposing front doors. The moat glowed an eerie, magical neon green.

"I don't think we should cross," Emily said, leaning towards the swirling mist. "I've had enough of bridges . . . Plus, are we just going to ring the doorbell when we get there?"

"Let's try to find another way in," Azari agreed, shivering. "That's the most evil-looking water I have ever seen."

"Worse than the Shadow Fountain?" Naida asked. She raised her hands towards the water and a magical glow surrounded her. Then she said, "I have good news."

"Go on – we could use some good news," Farran said.

"The moat's dry! The mist is just a magical illusion." Naida tossed a pebble down, and they heard it click against the bottom. It was a long drop from where they stood. "I am sensing a small trickling stream underneath the castle," Naida said.

"I bet it's an old mine. Water is an important part of mining, and these castles used to be built over some really big treasures!"

Azari told them. "We can sneak in through the tunnels. But . . . how will we get down there?"

"Aira could have built us something." Emily sighed. They felt Aira's absence with every step along their journey. Emily hoped they'd see her again soon.

"I can handle this," Farran said, pulling vines from the nearby forest and using his magic to twist them together into a swinging ladder. He dropped it over the side of the moat. "I made the ladder, so I'll go first," he said, stepping down on to it.

"We'll be right behind you!" Naida assured him. They watched as Farran disappeared into the mist.

Azari was about to follow when she saw the look the fire dragon was giving her. "Zonya can't come – she's too big to fit where we're going." She blew the dragon a fiery kiss. "See you later!" The fire dragon raised her head, spread her wings, and flew away.

When they all reached the bottom of the moat, Emily and the elves found the mine entrance and dashed inside, following the shallow stream Naida had heard. It was dark in the tunnels, but the walls glittered with precious stones, almost like stars. Emily thought it was beautiful. She told the others, "It's like the view from the inn!"

"Too bad it's under an evil castle run by an evil elf," Azari said.

"Yeah, too bad," Emily agreed with a chuckle.

They came to a fork in the tunnel, and everyone stopped, uncertain. "Let me see the book," Emily said. She quickly found the information they needed. "*Through crystal lights, a track runs fast,"* she read. *"Its cart will reach the castle at last . . ."*

"I see carts over there!" Farran pointed the way.

Suddenly, they all heard a *crack*. The third egg was hatching!

"Look at that!" Farran said, watching the baby emerge in the basket. "A baby earth dragon!" It looked sad, and wiggled around. Farran immediately gestured to Emily. "You have the magic touch," he said. Emily grinned and approached the baby. He saw Emily's glowing medallion and settled down.

"I hope we're getting closer to the dragon queen!" Naida said.

Emily agreed. Moving quickly with the baby dragons and the ever-trickling hourglass wasn't easy. She was sure they were all glad of a ride now. The old mining carts were on a rusted track that led deeper into the tunnels. They jumped in to one and were off . . .

"It's like a roller coaster!" Emily exclaimed as they went up and down steep hills, zooming around corners so fast they were all crushed to the cart's side.

"A what?" Naida asked.

"I'll explain later!" Emily shrieked as the cart flew around the final curve, coming to a stop in front of a mysterious door.

"Woo! That was wild!" Azari said. "Let's do it again!"

"No thanks." Farran's face was as green as his clothes.

They all piled out of the cart, and it zipped back up the tracks on its own.

"Aira would love those carts," Farran said in a soft voice. "She'd want to know exactly how they worked."

"Hopefully we'll tell her all about it soon," Emily said.

She stepped up to the door, feeling nervous as she reached out for the knob. "Ready?"

She opened the door.

Chapter 9
Trapped

The room they entered was so beautiful, Emily wondered if maybe they'd gone through a portal! It was dim, but she could see glinting silver and gold, and sparkling green crystals. It was like walking into a treasure chest.

A small stream flowed through the room. The trickling sound was soothing, yet Emily knew how much evil lurked there. Just like at the Shadow Fountain, looks could be deceiving.

She heard the rattle of chains. "The dragon queen must be nearby!"

"Here we go . . ." Azari pressed up against the wall. They needed to stay hidden for as long as possible.

"Shhh . . ." Naida warned as they tiptoed towards the dragon's cries.

SQUEAK!

"Oops! Sorry!" Farran looked to see what he'd stepped on. It was a cat's toy. "Weird," he said. "Hopefully the witch didn't – "

Suddenly, a giant chandelier lit up, revealing a throne beneath it . . . and the elf witch.

Emily caught her breath. Farran jumped as a black cat brushed past his legs, snatching the toy and running over to the witch.

"Welcome to my humble abode. I've been expecting you!" the witch said. She held up a turquoise dragon egg covered in silver glitter. "Aw, how sweet! You've brought me dragon babies to add to my collection. They're not doing so well, are they?"

It was the truth. The hourglass was nearly empty, and the dragon babies were weak and whining. "They need to be with their mother!" Emily said.

"Well, why didn't you say so?" The elf witch cackled. "I can arrange that!"

She raised her arms, and sparks flashed across the room. The baby dragons were ripped out of the girls' arms and floated high up into the air.

"Nooooo!" Emily screamed, leaping upward. But she couldn't reach them.

The elf witch waved her hands, and the dragon queen appeared behind her, roaring in fear and anger, chained up inside a magic force-field cage. The dragon pulled and thrashed, but the magical bonds held.

"Tsk, tsk, such a moody mummy," the witch said, grinning. She created another glowing force-field cage, and she forced the dragon babies into it with a roll of her hands. The dragon queen could see her children, but could not reach them.

Emily had never heard a sound as terrible as the one the dragon queen was making. It was pure despair. Emily's own heart felt like it might shatter.

In a blink, the witch appeared in front of Emily, studying her. "You're no elf," she said.

"Free the queen," Emily demanded, glaring at the witch. "She doesn't belong to you!" Instinctively, Emily raised her medallion.

It seemed to help the dragon queen as much as it had her babies – she calmed down noticeably. Emily also noticed that the dragon queen was wearing a necklace as well. How strange!

"It's so cute that you think you have a chance against my powers," the witch told Emily. "By the way, you might want to cover up those ears. I mean, ew."

Emily rolled her eyes and Azari said, "We like her ears just the way they are."

The witch snorted and then disappeared in a puff of green smoke.

"Where'd she go?" Farran said, looking around.

Suddenly, the elf witch reappeared at the back of the room. She was still holding the turquoise egg.

"I'll just put this on the roof to keep it away

from you," the witch called. "Go back to the forest, elfies, and play with your plants. Dragons are a witch's game!"

"We're not going anywhere till you release the dragon queen!" Azari said threateningly, but the witch was gone again.

"Where are the stairs?" Naida asked. But before they found a way to the roof, the witch reappeared in the room beside them. She looked amused. "Silly elves." She looked at each of them in turn. Everyone glared back.

"Wait . . . I feel like I'm missing something," the witch muttered. "Where's the last egg?"

Emily and the elves exchanged glances, making a silent vow not to tell her about the egg still with Aira.

The witch raised her hands once more. The room fell into shadow, followed by a bright flash of light that threw Emily and the elves backward across the room. They tumbled into one another, skidding into the furthest wall.

"Ouch!" Farran exclaimed. His head had banged hard against the wall. Azari helped him up.

"Where is the egg?" the elf witch screamed, aiming another blast at them. "Give me the last egg, or I'll imprison you all!"

This time, the elves were ready to use their magic. Farran swept vines off the wall, swirling them toward the witch to entrap her.

But the witch dodged away.

Naida took water from the mine stream and hurled a swirling orb of water across the room.

The cat and the witch both managed to dive under it.

Taking fire from a wall torch, Azari pitched a flaming ball at the elf witch. "Take that!"

She missed.

Emily saw how things were going, and said, "Everyone has to work together! Unite the magic!"

They quickly moved into a row, pooling their elemental energy as best they could, but it still wasn't enough. The elf witch closed in on the group, pressing another green force field towards them. The elves were unable to move.

Farran moaned. "Aira . . . We need Aira."

Emily felt her heart sink.

Suddenly, a huge gust of wind blasted open a castle window.

Aira soared in on the back of the wind dragon!

"AIRA!" they cheered. Emily was so relieved. She'd hoped beyond hope that Aira was okay, but it was wonderful to see her in person!

Even more good news followed – right behind Aira were the Sky Captain on the earth dragon, and the Dragon Trainer on the water dragon!

Finally, with a blast of fiery steam, the fire dragon also landed in the centre of the room. Her wing had already started to heal.

"Wow!" Emily exclaimed. There was so much joy in the room . . . but no time to rejoice.

The elf witch was so startled that she lost some of her control, and the elves could move again.

Aira leapt off the wind dragon and ran to hug her friends. "Gust is the best wind dragon!" she told them.

The Dragon Trainer and Sky Captain faced the witch. "Not so brave now, are we?" the Sky Captain said, laughing.

"Let's free those dragons!" Emily yelled.

"It's really good to be back," Aira said, leaping into action.

Everyone circled the witch, and the dragons swooped overhead.

"Get away from me!" the witch shouted. She sounded scared, but Emily noticed a hint of a smile.

"Something's wrong . . ." She shivered.

"What do you mean?" Azari looked over at her.

"I don't know . . . but it feels like it might be a trap!" She looked up and saw they were directly under the sparkling chandelier, which was starting to emit a green light. "Stay back! Go back!" Emily warned her friends, but it was too late. They were all trapped together in a force field, which pushed them to the other end of the room.

The elf witch waved her arm and magically took the last baby dragon from Aira's bag.

"Noooo!" Aira cried. It was the baby water dragon. The elf witch smirked at her, then threw her into the force field with her siblings.

"She's got all four baby dragons!" Emily exclaimed.

"She'll control the dragon queen," Aira said softly.

"She'll be able to take over Elvendale!" Farran moaned.

"And no dragon will ever trust an elf again!" Azari blinked back tears as the witch laughed.

"They're not going to make it!" Naida showed the hourglass. It was nearly empty.

"They'll be okay," the witch said. "That is, if their mother does what I say . . ." She cackled in a way that made Emily feel sick.

The dragon queen howled.

Emily sank to the floor, her head in her hands. She'd never felt so much sorrow and pain.

There was nothing else to do.

They'd lost.

Chapter 10

United in Magic

The black cat glared at them from outside the force field.

Azari whispered to Emily. "How are we going to get out of here?"

Emily didn't know. This was worse than the nightmare that had brought her to Elvendale. Her head hurt and she felt like she was going to cry. They couldn't let the elf witch win. There had to be a way . . .

Emily's mind started to clear. "Aira's here. We *can* do something!" A plan began to form. "Let's combine everyone's magic again! There's more of us now. Here – hold hands."

"Emily's right – let's kick some witch butt together!" Farran said. He took Aira's hand, and they all formed a chain, facing the witch.

"On three," Azari said, and counted down. They raised their hands together.

The air sparked with magic. A powerful beam of white light shot from them . . . and pierced the force field.

"Yes!" Emily cried, relieved. They leapt through one by one.

Unfortunately, the force field only stayed open long enough for Emily and the elves to rush through – the dragons, the Sky Captain, and the trainer were still trapped. But Emily felt the power shifting. She followed Azari towards the elf witch.

The witch blasted them with a bolt of magical lightning. "You fools! Just surrender now, and stop wasting my time."

With their powers combined, the elves managed to deflect the blast. But Emily knew they couldn't go on like this.

"The medallion," the Dragon Trainer shouted to her from beyond the force field. She recalled what he'd said to her at the school. *"You have a very important role in reuniting elves and dragons . . ."*

Energized, Emily stepped out in front of the others.

"Stop!" Aira cried.

But Emily didn't turn back. She walked straight towards the witch, her medallion glowing turquoise and gold.

When the witch blasted magic right at her, she didn't flinch. She thought about her mum, her dad, Grandmother, her friends, the dragons . . . the love she had for them made her strong and brave. She fiercely wanted to protect the dragons and her friends, and do what was needed to keep them all safe. She stepped closer and closer to the elf witch.

This time, the witch looked truly afraid. Emily held the medallion high above her head. The dragon queen roared, and magic burst through Emily's medallion.

The elves began cautiously approaching as it became clear the witch was losing strength. Emily glanced up and saw the chandelier directly above her and the witch. It swayed and glowed with an eerie light. Then Emily spotted a chain leading down from the fixture to the wall.

Now was her chance to trap the witch! She ran to where the chain was attached and gave it a huge kick.

"Aaaaaaaaiiieiieeee!" the witch's voice resonated through the entire castle as the chandelier fell, trapping her in her own force field.

"Emily, look out!" the Sky Captain shouted as the chandelier exploded. The cat scampered to safety, but the witch shrieked as she turned into a cloud of sparkling green dust. The dust cloud was clearly trying to escape, and zoomed around the room – everyone stood frozen in place, afraid to interfere. Finally, the dust zipped out through an open window.

The witch's magic dissolved with a hiss of smoke. All the force fields disappeared, and the dragon queen's chain burst open. Everyone was free!

As the babies rushed to their mother, Emily and the elves ran towards the other dragons, hugging their enormous legs with joy.

They'd done it!

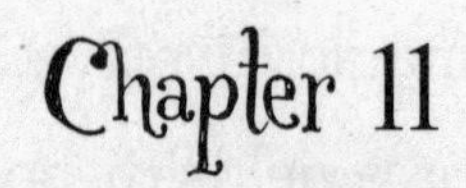

Chapter 11

The Last Egg

The castle was transforming in the most amazing ways. A pearlescent light swept through the rooms, removing all the darkness and bad feeling. Everyone cheered.

"The evil is gone!" Azari exclaimed.

"Emily, you're a hero! You did it!" The Dragon Trainer lifted her up in excitement.

"We all did it!" Emily cried, beaming.

"I'm glad we could make it in time to help,"

the Sky Captain said. She explained how there had been another forest fire near the Dragon Sanctuary, which the trainer had called her to help with. "And then Aira and the wind dragon showed up, and . . ."

Azari chuckled. "And now everything is back the way it should be!"

"Yes!" Emily exclaimed, turning towards the dragon queen and her babies. It was then that Emily realized that not only had her medallion been glowing in colours that matched the dragon queen's scales, the dragon queen's pendant was also glowing. "Wow," Emily said, sighing.

The dragon queen snuggled her babies close, and Emily was glad to see that they all looked much healthier. The hourglass was forgotten on the floor.

But there was something in the dragon queen's eyes that concerned Emily. "Hang on . . . we almost forgot the turquoise egg!" she realized. "There's still one more baby!"

Leaving the others behind, Emily hurried to the roof. She spotted the glittering egg right away. The cat had reached it first, and sat in front, hissing as Emily advanced.

Just then, the dragon queen rose over the castle wall!

"Hi!" Emily said, welcoming her. "You get your egg! I'll take care of the cat."

Emily stomped her feet and made shooing motions at the cat while the queen scooped up the egg and ducked back down into the castle.

"Sorry, kitty. Good beats evil!" Emily grinned as the cat snarled at her. She ran back down the stairs.

The Dragon Trainer solemnly addressed the group. "Emily, you and your friends have rebuilt the trust between elves and dragons, and have brought harmony to Elvendale. Thank you." Then he broke into a huge smile.

Emily remembered how tense and unhappy he'd been when they first met him at the school. Things had definitely changed!

The Sky Captain had retrieved the ancient book, and was eager to get moving. "Way to go, everyone! Now let's ride us some dragons! Though I wish I had my airship. I'm not a big fan of dragon-travel." She whispered to Emily, "I get a little dragon-sick . . ."

Emily laughed. The Sky Captain had a weakness, just like the rest of them!

It was time to go. But before they left, the

dragon queen bent low toward Emily, offering her thanks. Emily reached out and touched her head . . . and the queen's amulet lit up, joining Emily's medallion in a brilliant blaze. Emily felt a swell of love and friendship. And suddenly, in her heart, she knew the queen's name: Elandra. She smiled at her new friend.

Then Elandra and her babies all bowed low to Emily and the elves. Emily was surprised and overwhelmed with joy.

Azari, Aira, Naida and Farran climbed on to their elemental dragons. The Sky Captain doubled up behind Farran, and the Dragon Trainer got behind Aira.

Emily turned towards the dragon queen, who crouched down invitingly. Emily climbed on to her back – along with all the dragon babies, and the last egg! She wanted this happiness to linger, so she moved slowly. It was the best feeling. They'd succeeded! It hadn't been easy, but Emily was so proud of what they'd accomplished.

Just then, the turquoise egg began to crack.

"Oooh!" Emily exclaimed, and everyone looked over.

"What kind of dragon can it be?" Naida asked. "All the elements are already here." She glanced over at the happy wind, fire, water and earth dragon babies.

The eggshell dropped away, revealing a bright blue, white and gold dragon.

"Of course," Emily said. "A baby dragon queen!"

"She looks just like her mother!" Azari said with a warm smile.

The baby queen nestled into Emily's lap.

She held on to the dragon queen's scales as it lifted up and into the sky.

"This way!" Azari pointed towards the Dragon School. "These dragons are going home!"

Chapter 12

Back Home

They landed at the Dragon School to find that there was a celebration waiting for them! Elves from near and far had heard the news that the dragons were all free and trusted elves again.

Emily couldn't stop smiling as she leapt down into the training arena and was swept up in a sea of elves offering her food and drink. She ate a piece of cake that was such a strange colour, she didn't know how to describe it. It was delicious!

There was even a band of elves playing a very catchy tune on musical instruments that Emily didn't recognize. The Dragon Trainer jumped down from his ride and started singing and dancing along, making Emily remember what she'd thought when she'd first seen him – maybe he could have been a famous singer if he wasn't a Dragon Trainer! He was really good.

This was an amazing party.

After the song was over, the trainer came over to Emily.

"You were pretty awesome today," he said. "When you trapped the witch in her own force field . . . Wow!" He looked at her intently. "What kind of magic do you have, Emily from Another World?"

Emily shook her head. "None. I'm not magical."

He reached out and touched her medallion. "Is this the source of your power, then?"

"No," she admitted, though she wished the medallion would give her actual magical powers – that would be great. For a second, Emily wondered what kind of power she'd like to have: earth magic like Farran? Wind magic like Aira? She thought fire was too dangerous and she might set something ablaze by accident. Or water?

She did have a theory about what had happened, though. "I think that my necklace was able to connect to the amulet the dragon queen wore. That's why I saw her image in my medallion before I knew anything about her, and why the necklace was able to calm her babies."

Farran and Aira were dancing nearby. "It's

still weird that a dragon wears a necklace," Farran said. "Not sure about that."

"Yeah," Emily said, touching the stone and wishing she knew all its secrets.

Azari, Naida and the Sky Captain gathered around as well, and for a few minutes, Emily was happily lost in her circle of friends. They all danced some more, and the next thing Emily knew, the sun was going down.

"I need to get back home," she told her friends. "That means going to Skyra's castle." Last time she'd visited Elvendale, she'd gone home through a portal guarded by the elf Skyra.

"We'll take you—" Aira began.

"And on the way, you can tell us about roller coasters," Naida added, smiling.

"You've got a deal—" The sudden flapping of wings made Emily look up.

"It's the dragon queen!" Azari cheered. The dragon looked so happy; at her side was a parade of her babies.

"She's come to take you to Skyra's castle," the Dragon Trainer said. "Or anywhere you want to go. We'll take care of the babies here until you get back!"

"I'll just go to the castle," Emily told him with a laugh.

Her friends gathered around her, forming a tight circle. It was a big group hug, just like when she'd arrived. In fact, Farran pushed too hard from the side and everyone toppled to the ground again! They laughed, but Emily knew that inside, they all felt like she did – they were sad she was leaving. It was so hard to say goodbye.

Emily climbed on to the dragon queen's back.

"Have a safe flight!" the Sky Captain called.

As the dragon rose into the air, Emily looked down at Azari, Farran, Aira and Naida. She waved.

It had been a challenging journey, but because they'd worked together, they'd succeeded. It was quite an adventure! They'd kept the dragon babies safe and reunited them with their mother, and had restored balance to the relationship between elves and dragons. The elf witch was gone, and Elvendale was safe.

Emily raised her chin and let the wind whip through her hair. She clasped Grandmother's medallion in her hands, then shouted down to her friends, "See you soon!"

They shouted back, "Don't be gone long!"

"I won't! I promise!" Emily smiled as she soared towards home.